Gratitude Seeds

Written and Illustrated by
Sarah Elizabeth Olson

ISBN 9798387593680

Dedicated to Anyah, Aubrey & Axel

I am grateful for you everyday.

As the warm sun rose over the farm,
the rooster called out his cock-a-doodle-doo,
the yellow sunflowers popped up their heads
and the ducks waddled to the pond.

Bella the butterfly flitted over
the farm and found a perfect
soft place to land...
in Johnny's sunflower petals.

As Bella nestled in, she began to tell Johnny, the sunflower, how she woke up feeling especially grumpy...her wing tip was bent, her antenna was crooked and her mood was just plain grouchy.

Johnny listened and gave an understanding nod and smile.

Johnny told her, "on my grumpiest of days I try to plant as many gratitude seeds as I can."

"What are gratitude seeds?" asked Bella.

"Instead of focusing on what is going wrong, I focus on the things in my day that make me happy, that make me laugh and that make my heart warm and fuzzy. These are gratitude seeds - the things that I am grateful for. Before long, I have a harvest of happiness instead of grumpiness."

Bella flew away thinking of what Johnny had said.
"Maybe I can get rid of my grumpy feelings
if I plant some of my own gratitude seeds,"
she thought.

As Bella flew through the woods, she smelled the blossoms on the trees and the fresh pine.

"I'm grateful for these beautiful woods and the sights and the smells as I fly through them."

As Bella focused on the beautiful scenery around her, her crooked antenna felt a little straighter.

Soon Bella found herself flying over the water and she couldn't help but notice how peaceful it was.

Bella found a spot to rest and thought
about how grateful she was for the
peaceful place to sit and reflect.

As she quietly sat on the rock
she noticed that her wing tip
didn't feel bent any more.

Bella flitted past mountains and noticed how majestic they were; she noticed the detail in the trees and how the sun seemed to make them sparkle.

"I am grateful for the sunshine, the fresh air, the mountains and the trees," thought Bella.

Bella felt the lift in her wings and the shift in her attitude.

Bella reached the tree grove where she was surrounded by her friends and family.

"I am thankful for each one of my friends and family members," thought Bella and her heart began to feel warm and fuzzy.

As the moon came up and the stars twinkled in the velvety sky, Bella realized she had one more gratitude seed to plant.

"I am grateful for this beautiful night with the moon and the shining stars," thought Bella as she happily flitted home.

As Bella nestled into her soft, flowery bed
for the night, she remembered all of the gratitude
seeds she planted that day...

Bella planted seeds of gratitude for the beautiful woods
and the sights and smells they provided,
for a peaceful spot to rest and reflect by the water,
for sunshine, fresh air, mountains and trees,
for family and friends,
and for the shining moon and stars...

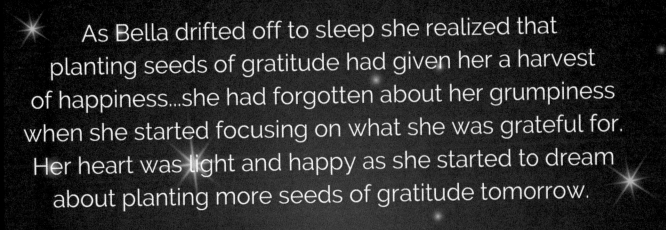

As Bella drifted off to sleep she realized that planting seeds of gratitude had given her a harvest of happiness...she had forgotten about her grumpiness when she started focusing on what she was grateful for. Her heart was light and happy as she started to dream about planting more seeds of gratitude tomorrow.

What seeds of gratitude can you plant today to reap a

harvest of happiness!

"Rejoice always, pray without ceasing, give thanks in all circumstances." 1 Thessalonians 5:16-17

About the Author

Sarah Elizabeth Olson lives with her husband, Johnny, and their three kids in Minnesota. They love sunflowers and spreading sunshine to others through their community outreach project, the Sunshine Foundation of America.

Sarah is passionate about her faith, family, fitness and of course, writing!